To L.M.A., J.M.A., and K.R.A., the loves of my life
—J.J.A.

For Dan, the worm of my dreams
—M.C.

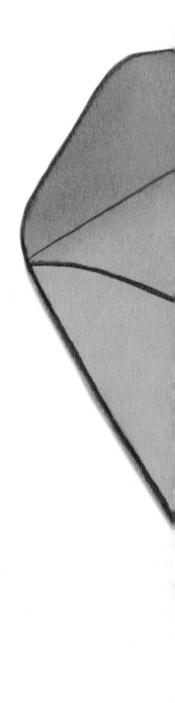

Balzer + Bray is an imprint of HarperCollins Publishers.

Worm Loves Worm

Text copyright © 2016 by J. J. Austrian. Illustrations copyright © 2016 by Mike Curato
All rights reserved. Manufactured in China.

ISBN 978-0-06-238633-5

The artist used pencil and Photoshop to create the illustrations for this book.
Typography by Martha Rago
15 16 17 18 19 SCP 10 9 8 7 6 5 4 3 2 1
❖
First Edition

WORM Loves WORM

J. J. Austrian ♡ Mike Curato

Balzer + Bray
an imprint of HarperCollinsPublishers

Worm loves Worm.
"Let's be married,"
says Worm to Worm.

"Yes!" answers Worm.

"Let's be married."

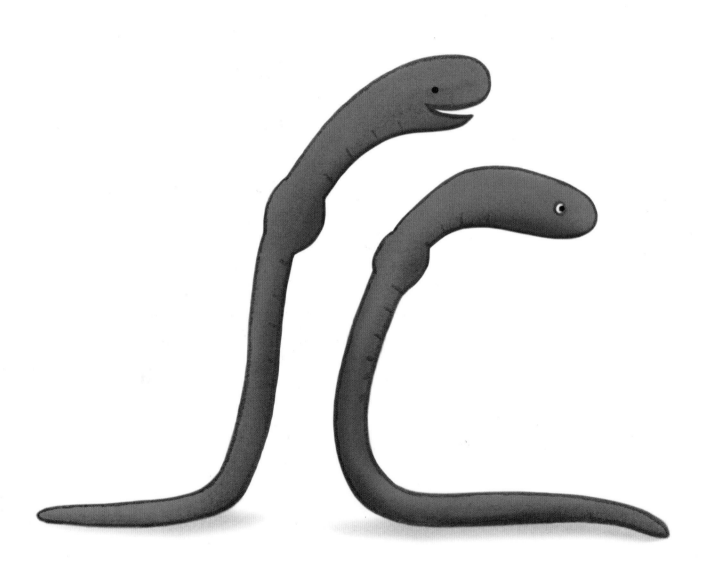

"Wait!" says Cricket.
"You'll need someone
to marry you. That's how
it's always been done.
I'll marry you."

"Now can we be married?"
asks Worm.

"Wait!" says Beetle. "You've got to have a best beetle. Naturally, that would be me."

"Now can we be married?"
asks Worm.

"Wait! Wait! Wait!"
say the Bees. "You need
bride's bees. Can we
be the bride's bees?
Please? Please? Please?"

"Yes," says Worm. "Now can we be married?"

"You'll need to get rings to wear on your fingers," says Cricket. "That's how it's always been done."

"But we don't have fingers," says Worm.

"We can wear them
like belts," says Worm.

"Wonderful," says Worm.
"Now we can be married."

"Just make sure to have a band so we can dance," says Beetle.

"But we don't have feet to dance with," says Worm.

"We can just wiggle around,"
says Worm. "Like this."

"Fun," says Worm. "Now
we can be married."

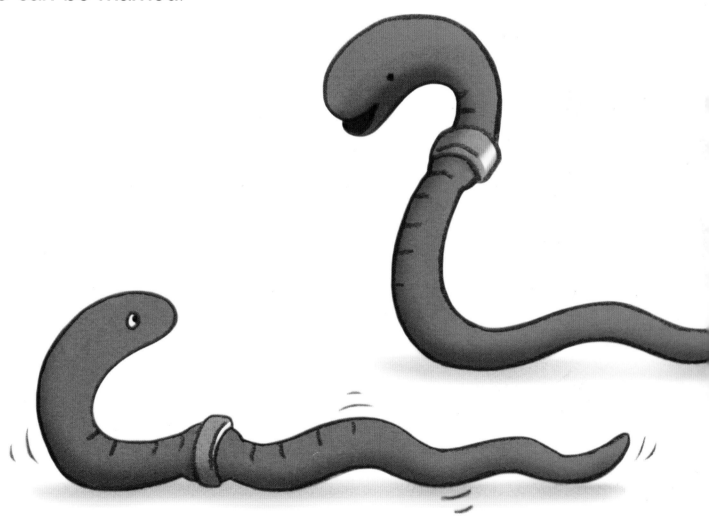

"But you still need
a white dress,
a tuxedo, a top hat,
lots and lots of flowers,
and a cake with frosting,"
say the Bees.

"But we don't have heads
for hats," says Worm.
"Or hands to hold flowers."

"And we only eat dirt,"
says Worm.

"Wait!" says Spider.
"I can attach the hat
and flowers to you
with my sticky web."

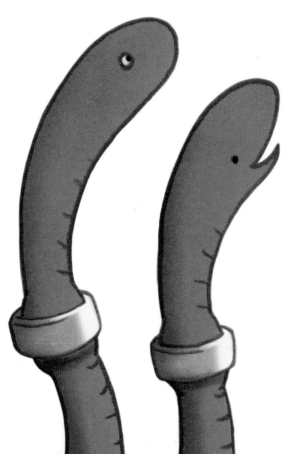

"Thank you,"
say Worm and Worm.

"But who will eat the cake?"
ask the Bees.

"I can eat the cake along
with Cricket and Beetle,"
says Spider.

"What did you say?" ask Cricket and Beetle.

"Nothing," says Spider with a smile.

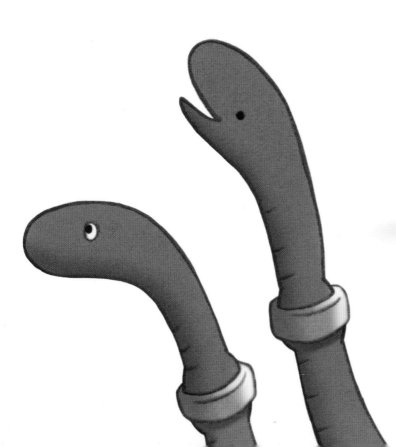

"Now we can be married," says Worm.

"But which one of you
is the bride?" ask the Bees.
"How can we be bride's bees
if we don't know who the
bride is?"

"I can be the bride," says Worm.

"I can, too," says Worm.

"But one of you has got to be the groom, or how can I be best beetle?" asks Beetle.

"I can be the groom," says Worm.

"I can, too," says Worm. "We can be both."

"Amazing," says Spider.

"Really?" ask Beetle
and the Bees.

"Wait!" says Cricket. "That isn't how it's always been done."

"Then we'll just change
how it's done," says Worm.

"Yes," says Worm.

And so they were married...

because Worm loves Worm.

To L.M.A., J.M.A., and K.R.A., the loves of my life
—J.J.A.

For Dan, the worm of my dreams
—M.C.

Balzer + Bray is an imprint of HarperCollins Publishers.

Worm Loves Worm

Text copyright © 2016 by J. J. Austrian. Illustrations copyright © 2016 by Mike Curato

oks, a division of HarperCollins Publishers, 195 Broadway, New York, NY 10007.
www.harpercollinschildrens.com

ISBN 978-0-06-238633-5

pencil and Photoshop to create the illustrations for this book.
Typography by Martha Rago
6 17 18 19 SCP 10 9 8 7 6 5 4 3 2 1
❖
First Edition

WORM *Loves* WORM

J. J. Austrian ♡ Mike Curato

Balzer + Bray
an imprint of HarperCollinsPublishers

Worm loves Worm.
"Let's be married,"
says Worm to Worm.

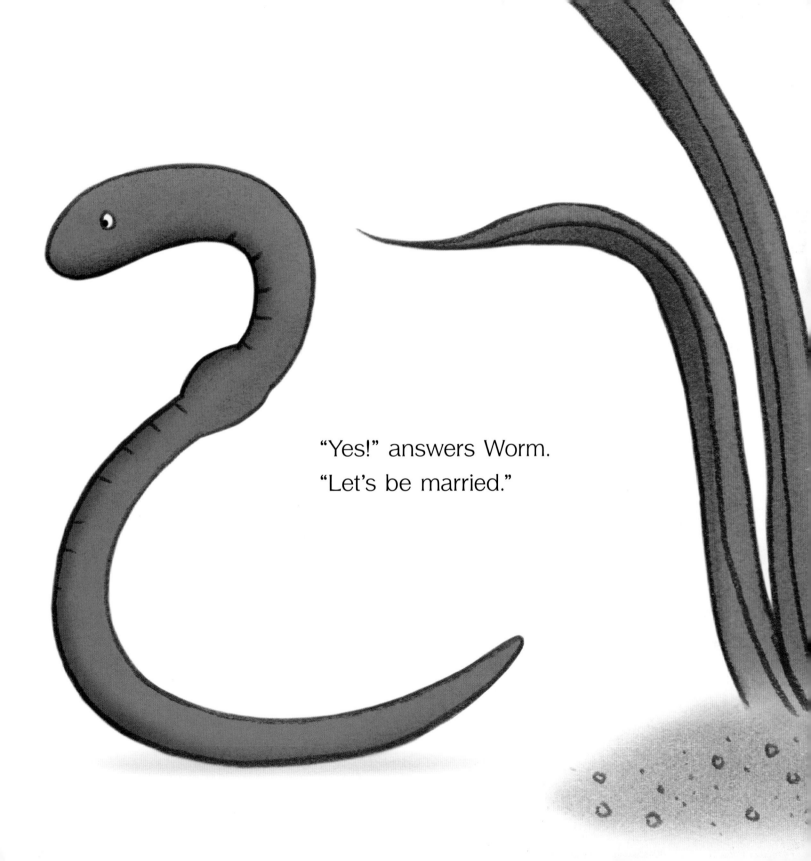

"Yes!" answers Worm.

"Let's be married."

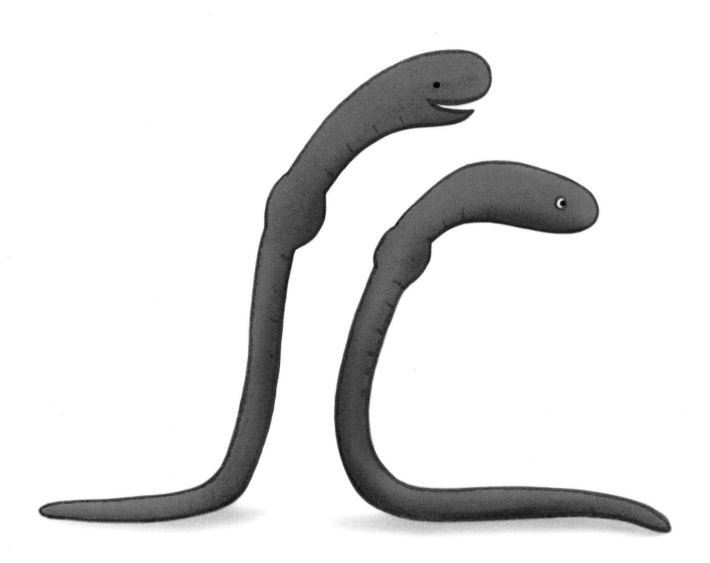

"Wait!" says Cricket.
"You'll need someone
to marry you. That's how
it's always been done.
I'll marry you."

"Now can we be married?" asks Worm.

"Wait!" says Beetle. "You've got to have a best beetle. Naturally, that would be me."

"Now can we be married?"
asks Worm.

"Wait! Wait! Wait!"
say the Bees. "You need
bride's bees. Can we
be the bride's bees?
Please? Please? Please?"

"Yes," says Worm. "Now can we be married?"

"You'll need to get rings to wear on your fingers," says Cricket. "That's how it's always been done."

"But we don't have fingers," says Worm.

"We can wear them
like belts," says Worm.

"Wonderful," says Worm.
"Now we can be married."

"Just make sure to have a band so we can dance," says Beetle.

"But we don't have feet to dance with," says Worm.

"We can just wiggle around,"
says Worm. "Like this."

"Fun," says Worm. "Now
we can be married."

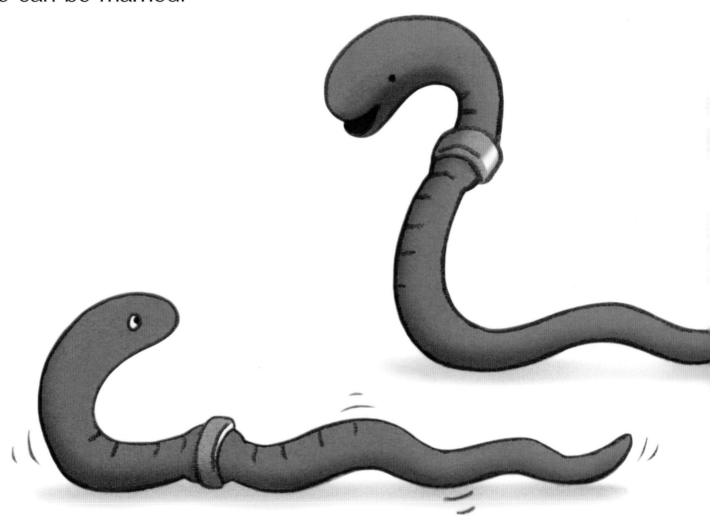

"But you still need
a white dress,
a tuxedo, a top hat,
lots and lots of flowers,
and a cake with frosting,"
say the Bees.

"But we don't have heads
for hats," says Worm.
"Or hands to hold flowers."

"And we only eat dirt,"
says Worm.

"Wait!" says Spider.
"I can attach the hat
and flowers to you
with my sticky web."

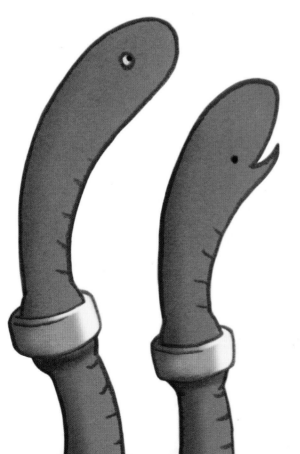

"Thank you,"
say Worm and Worm.

"But who will eat the cake?"
ask the Bees.

"I can eat the cake along
with Cricket and Beetle,"
says Spider.

"What did you say?" ask
Cricket and Beetle.

"Nothing," says Spider
with a smile.

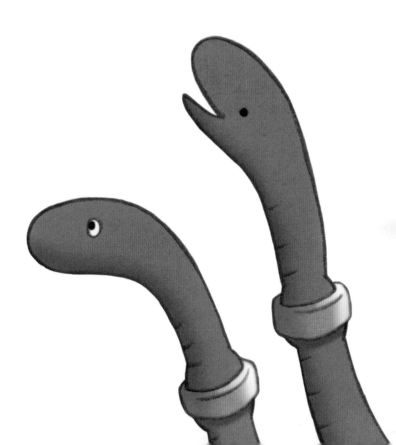

"Now we can be married,"
says Worm.

"But which one of you
is the bride?" ask the Bees.
"How can we be bride's bees
if we don't know who the
bride is?"

"I can be the bride,"
says Worm.

"I can, too," says Worm.

"But one of you has got to be the groom, or how can I be best beetle?" asks Beetle.

"I can be the groom," says Worm.

"I can, too," says Worm. "We can be both."

"Amazing," says Spider.

"Really?" ask Beetle
and the Bees.

"Wait!" says Cricket. "That isn't how it's always been done."

"Then we'll just change
how it's done," says Worm.

"Yes," says Worm.

And so they were married...

because Worm loves Worm.